HOORAY FOR OUR HEROES!

by Sarah Albee • illustrated by Tom Brannon

Random House 🏠 New York

The publishers wish to thank Tom Brannon for volunteering his time and talent to create the new cover art for this special book.

Hello there, everybodee! It is I, your furry superhero pal, Super Grover! Today I am going to tell you what the word "hero" means. A hero is someone who you see in comic books and cartoons. Heroes are make-believe.

First of all, a hero has a special uniform, similar to the outfit that I am wearing, with a cape on the back and a letter on the chest. I do not see anyone else wearing a hero uniform, do you?

And, of course, everyone knows that heroes have very large muscles and are very strong. No one around here is especially strong.

Heroes move with lightning speed. No one around here can do that.

Of course, heroes must also be able to fly. Aside from yours truly, no one around here can do that.

And heroes must be able to leap tall buildings in a single bound.

Heroes are famous. They are never the people that we see walking around our own neighborhoods.

My best friend is my hero! He taught me how to ride a bike.

How would you know a hero if you saw one? That is a very good question! And I, Grover, will answer it for you. For starters, heroes definitely do not wear glasses.

And heroes do not just sit around, waiting for things to happen.

Heroes rescue people who need help. I do not see anyone around here being rescued, do you?

Heroes are people you look up to.

Heroes protect and defend.

I hope that now you understand what it means to be a hero. Thank you!

A Note for Parents and Kids

Tom Brannon created this book's cover art to celebrate some of the biggest heroes of the current health crisis: nurses and doctors who care for the sick, and the delivery people who bring food and other needed supplies.

All of today's essential workers are true heroes, and they are paving the way for a brighter tomorrow. They also include the people keeping grocery stores and drugstores stocked and running, the scientists working on cures and vaccines, the volunteers dedicated to helping any way they can, police officers, firefighters, and many, many others.

You can say thank you to the heroes in your neighborhood by:

- writing a card or letter
- painting a picture and hanging it in your window
- creating a sidewalk chalk message or drawing
- taking part in a community clap at the same time every day
- giving this book to an essential worker in your life

And don't forget to say . . .

HOORAY FOR OUR HEROES!

Thank You!